Artlist Collection
THE DOG

Leader of the Pack

W9-CHE-127

By Howie Dewin

SCHOLASTIC INC.

New York   Toronto   London   Auckland   Sydney

Mexico City   New Delhi   Hong Kong   Buenos Aires

For Callie

ISBN-13: 978-0-545-07858-0
ISBN-10: 0-545-07858-X

12 11 10 9 8 7 6 5 4 3 2   08 09 10 11 12/0

Designed by Angela Jun
Printed in the U.S.A.
First printing, September 2008

★ Meet Mugsy ★

I need a home.

He's a two-year-old Pug adopted by twelve-year-old Tessa. Mugsy is kind. Mugsy is loving. Unfortunately, Mugsy wasn't treated nicely where he used to live. He got punished for almost anything. That's why he's a nervous dog now. But Tessa and her mom don't understand. They think Mugsy is just a badly trained dog. That's why, starting today, Mugsy is being enrolled at Top Dog Obedience School. . . .

Chapter 1
Welcome to Top Dog

"Come on, Mugsy! Come here, boy!" The Pug dog, small and wrinkled, stared at the young girl calling his name. He did not move.

Mugsy was telling himself to move, but his little Pug body was not listening. His stubby little legs twitched, but it looked like he was just dancing.

"Mugsy!" Tessa snapped. "Come!"

Tessa was always kind to Mugsy, and he really wanted to please her. She was in charge of making sure he had his meals, enough exercise, and lots of visits to the backyard. But right now, she was getting frustrated.

"We are going OUT, Mugsy!" she pleaded.

Oh, no! thought Mugsy as his feet went out from under him. *That is no way to get me to move. When will she learn that "OUT" is a scary word?*

Mugsy's heart sank as he scrambled back to

his feet. Tessa thought he was being bad. She didn't understand he was afraid of just about everything that moved. Even an unexpected breeze could scare Mugsy.

"Mugsy!" Tessa said in a low voice. "You are coming whether you want to or not!"

She picked him up, put him in her shoulder bag, and headed out on her bicycle.

As Tessa began to pedal, Mugsy whimpered. Words flashed through his Pug brain: *Too fast! Not natural! Dogs are not supposed to move so fast!*

Finally, the bike slowed.

"Okay, MugsyPup," he heard Tessa say, "here we are."

One paw in front of another, he said to himself. He followed Tessa into the building.

"Welcome to Top Dog!" A lady was talking to them. She sat behind a desk just inside the door.

I wonder what this place is, Mugsy thought.

"Your name?" the nice lady asked Tessa.

"Tessa Anderson, and this is Mugsy," Tessa said.

But Mugsy wasn't listening.

"Mugsy!" Tessa said loudly.

Mugsy jumped straight up. He came down crooked and crashed into the lady's desk.

"He's a daydreamer," Tessa explained to the woman behind the desk.

"Straight through the doors in the back," said the woman. Then she stood and looked down at Mugsy. "Welcome to Top Dog Training School, Mugsy! Your first obedience class is just moments away!"

Mugsy's eyes grew larger. It felt like his eyeballs might fall out of his head! *Top Dog!?* *Obedience class!?* His jaw dropped.

Were you talking to me?

"It's time to learn a few rules, Mugsy," Tessa said cheerfully.

Mugsy's knees locked. His belly brushed the floor. He started to pant so hard that some people laughed and pointed.

Tessa picked him up. "Mugsy," she whispered as they headed toward the door. "We have to make this work, or Mom says we'll have to find another home for you. She says you can't have a dog who doesn't obey. So please . . . !"

Tessa reached for the doorknob, but a poster taped to the door caught her eye. "Look, Mugsy, this is going to be fun. It says there will be a competition with trophies at the end of the term!"

It just keeps getting worse! thought Mugsy.

Tessa pulled open the door. They entered a huge room. It was filled with loud, excited dogs.

And worse and worse! He moaned.

Mugsy started panting even harder. This was the scariest place he had ever been! But it was about to get a lot scarier. From behind Mugsy, a thundering voice rang out.

"MOVE!" was all it said, over and over. "MOVE! MOVE! MOVE!"

He turned his body so he could look over Tessa's shoulder. That's when he let out a yelp.

Teeth! Claws! Huge! Loud! HELP! Those were the only words in Mugsy's head. This was turning out to be a very bad day.

The Pug breed originated in China more than 2,000 years ago.

Chapter 2
Girl's History of Dogs

"Look at all these nice dogs," whispered Tessa. She didn't notice the terrible beast behind them.

Look at all these different ways to be ripped to shreds, thought Mugsy. *What is that . . . thing behind us?*

Mugsy wished Tessa understood him. He wanted to know what had just entered the room. He really wanted Tessa to understand that they should go home!

"I'm Andy, and this is Thor," said the young boy with the monster. The boy talked to a man with a clipboard.

"Pit Bull?" asked the man with the clipboard.

"Yes, sir," the boy answered.

The man shook the boy's hand. "Welcome to Top Dog," he said.

Mugsy looked around. Nobody else looked as worried as he felt. He had heard about Pit Bulls, and it seemed like a bad idea to be this close to one. He was happy to see that Tessa at least looked a little worried.

"Don't worry," said the boy named Andy. He was talking to Tessa. "He's been mine since he was a puppy. We've always been really gentle with him. My dad trained him with the basic commands. He really is the sweetest dog you'll ever meet."

Tessa smiled.

Then why is he here? Mugsy wondered. *If he's so well-behaved, why is he here?*

It was like Tessa read his mind. She asked, "Then why do you have him in class?"

Mugsy wanted to hug her, but his arms were too short.

"He needs to get more exercise. The vet said he was getting a bit lazy." Andy laughed. "I thought this would be good for him. I understand a lot of the class takes place on the obstacle course."

An obsti-what? Mugsy wondered.

"Lie down, Thor," said Andy.

Thor slid forward on his front paws until he was lying down.

"Awww!" said Tessa.

Mugsy couldn't believe it! *Awww?* he thought. *Awwwww? The beast obeys one command, and you're in love?*

"He really is cute." Tessa giggled. "Say hello, Mugsy," she said. Suddenly, Tessa was lowering Mugsy to the floor.

DANGER! DANGER! DO NOT LOWER THE PUG! Mugsy was shouting, but all Tessa heard was a high-pitched squeak. His claws grabbed Tessa's sweater. He did not want his paws to touch the floor.

"Mugsy!" Tessa giggled.

No! Save me! His legs scrambled like he was running in midair.

As his feet touched the ground, he heard a voice.

"Pit Bull," the voice said.

Mugsy turned quickly. A tall, thin Boxer stood looking at Thor and Mugsy. "The Pit Bull is in the Mastiff group of dogs, which, oddly enough, so are you, Pug Boy," the Boxer said.

Mugsy looked at the Boxer. He wondered if she was crazy.

"Of course, there are some big differences between you. Like about a hundred pounds!" said the Boxer as she laughed.

Mugsy didn't think it was funny. His feet went out from under him again.

"Ah, stand up, kid. It's not so scary. You're safe here," said the Boxer.

Mugsy nodded slowly. He was grateful for the Boxer's kindness.

"What are *you*?" Mugsy asked.

"I'm a Boxer," she said proudly. "My name is Girl."

"Boxers aren't scary?" he asked in a whisper.

"No. We're too smart to be bullies! Besides, I belong to Frank."

"Who's Frank?" Mugsy spit out.

"Him." The Boxer pointed toward the school owner with the clipboard.

"I'll tell you a secret. I'm in the Mastiff group, too. I have even more in common with Thor than you do! Boxers and Pit Bulls both have some Bulldog blood in us."

Mugsy looked worried.

Girl touched her nose to Mugsy in friendship. "Don't worry," she said. "Remember? We're not bullies!"

GIRL

Girl Says

Boxers are stars of the show! Boxers have a proud history as circus and theater dogs. They were chosen to perform because they are good at doing tricks!

"So much can be explained by breeding," she said. "With my performance background, it's fitting that I should belong to the owner of Top Dog. But don't worry, I don't have a swelled head. The truth is, if I had a swelled head (which I don't), it would be because I'm smart and good-looking . . . not because I'm in charge of this whole place."

"That is interesting," Mugsy said. "But can you tell me how we'll be safe if that Pit Bull decides it's lunchtime and he's out of kibble?"

"Well, for starters," Girl said with a laugh, "I can hide in there!" She nodded toward a metal door. "I have one doggy door that goes into the room and one doggy door that goes out. It's safe. And the door is around the corner and down the hall. I know the way, and the Pit Bull doesn't."

"Please show *me* the way to the doggy door," Mugsy whimpered.

Girl didn't seem to hear him. She was looking toward the entrance.

"Oh, great," she said in an annoyed voice.

"What?" Mugsy said in a low whisper.

"German Shepherd," she said. "They are

so conceited. I've never met one who wasn't a snob."

"Hello," said the young woman with the German Shepherd. "I'm Adrienne, and this is Kiki," she said.

Kiki looked around the room. Her head and tail were both held high. Mugsy could see what Girl meant. It felt like she was looking down on everyone in the room.

KIKI

"Kiki went to a summer camp this year. The people there said she was great on the obstacle course. We decided she might like to take a class here." Adrienne talked loudly. It seemed she wanted everyone to hear how great her dog was.

"Very good," said Frank. "Take your place at the end of the line, please. We'll get started in a few moments."

Mugsy watched Kiki. The German Shepherd walked toward them on her way to the end of the line. She seemed to expect dogs and humans to step out of her way. Mugsy took a deep breath. Kiki was coming right toward Thor, who was lying on the floor. The Pit Bull watched the German Shepherd carefully. He didn't look like he was going to move.

"This should be interesting," Girl said.

Kiki walked directly up to Thor. "Excuse me!" she hissed.

"For what?" Thor growled.

Kiki glared at Thor. She mumbled something as she stepped over the Pit Bull's back legs.

"What?!" Thor snapped.

Kiki didn't repeat what she had mumbled. But Mugsy had heard her. She had said, "Pit Bulls are so stupid!" *Oh, oh, oh,* thought Mugsy. There was going to be trouble for sure! Sooner or later, Thor and Kiki were going to have it out!

"Girl?" Mugsy said in a squeak. He looked around. Girl was gone. All Mugsy heard was a flapping doggy door on the other side of the room.

Chapter 3
The First Day of School

"I'm HERE!" A screeching voice rang out from the entrance. "Let the party begin, Zach has arrived! Ta! Da!"

All heads turned. A crazy dog had arrived at school. He bounced up and down like a basketball. An old lady held his leash.

"I'm Zach! Oh, yeah! It's my birthday! Uh-huh! It's my birthday! Oh, yeah!"

"Zachy, dear," said the old woman. "Zachy, dear, hush now. We have to talk to the young man."

Zach started making little tiny steps with his feet. He looked like a tap dancer.

"Hello, young man," the woman said. "I'm here with little Zach. He might be registered under my name: Mrs. Egan."

"I have him right here," said Frank. "Zach the Jack Russell Terrier."

"Oh, yeah!" shouted Zach. "Uh-huh! I'm Zach! I'm a Jack! I'm Zach! I'm a Jack! Comin' attcha!"

"Zachy has a lot of energy," said Mrs. Egan with a smile.

"That's fine." Frank smiled back. "Take the last spot, please."

"This is great! This is swell! How do you do? What's your name?" Zach jumped and spun around. He tripped over a big sheepdog lying in the middle of the floor.

"Hey-hey, Mr. Furry! Deepest apologies! I so did not mean to do that! Whoo-hoo!"

Why am I here?

"Possibly Attention Deficit Disorder," Girl said. She had snuck up behind Mugsy again.

"Hey!" said Mugsy to Girl. "Where did you go? It got really scary here a minute ago!"

Girl Says

A Jack Russell Terrier is a big dog in little body. Jack Russells are spirited and fearless. After all, they were bred to dig foxes out of their dens! The key to a happy and obedient Jack Russell is an experienced owner who knows how to train a dog, because Jack Russells are not easy to train!

Girl ignored him. She just sat there with a little smile.

She's always smiling, Mugsy thought. *Must be a Boxer thing. Like I always look worried. Hey! Wait a minute, I am always worried.*

"Mugsy!" said Tessa. "Don't wander off. Class is about to begin."

Zach was bouncing up and down. "I'm in school! I'll be smart! I'll be cool!" He moved so quickly that Mugsy didn't realize how close he was to Thor. All of a sudden, he bounced right down on top of Thor.

The room went silent.

"Zachy, dear," said the old lady, "don't bounce on the big doggy's head."

Andy held tight to Thor's leash. The big dog barely moved. He just quietly growled, "You— are annoying. Get away from me."

Zach took three scoots back. He looked like he was tap dancing again. He moved to the end of the line, next to Kiki. He spoke more quietly.

"I'm Zach. I'm annoying. Yeah, I'm Zach. I'm annoying . . ."

Zach took his place next to Kiki. The German Shepherd bent down and whispered in Zach's ear. The Jack Russell leaped into the air. He seemed so pleased with what Kiki had said that he actually leaped right over Kiki!

★ ★ ★ ★ ★ ★

"Welcome," said Frank. He was standing in front of the class with his clipboard. "I'm happy to have such a mixed class. It's great when every-one comes with different abilities. Dogs are just like people. They can learn from one another."

Mugsy looked down the line. He wondered who he would learn from. Kiki was looking down the line, too. But she was just giving dirty looks to everyone.

Thor lay on the ground. Mugsy wondered if there was anything that made Thor look happy.

Probably just a good snack, he thought. *I hope he doesn't like Pug.*

Mugsy tried to keep his distance from Thor. He leaned in the other direction while they were practicing "sit." The leaning made it hard for him to obey. When Tessa said "sit," Mugsy would try. But the leaning made him fall down. Over and over, it happened.

At the other end, Zach never stopped talking. The only dog he didn't seem to bother was Kiki. That made no sense to Mugsy because everyone else seemed to annoy her! It seemed like Kiki was trying to get Zach to talk even more. She giggled at everything he said. She kept saying things like, "Really? Tell me more!"

Dogs are so weird, Mugsy thought.

Mugsy just wanted to disappear. But Tessa wouldn't let that happen. He looked down the line again.

Could anyone here be my friend? he wondered.

Zach was legally insane. Kiki was a mean snob. Girl was obsessed with herself. Thor was dangerous.

"Okay, everybody!" Frank finally said. "Great first class! We'll see you back here next week! Remember, daily practice!"

"Well, Mugsy," Tessa said, "wasn't it fun to be with so many other dogs?"

I wish I was home!

Mugsy stared up into Tessa's eyes. All he could think was: *I am so deeply misunderstood.*

She picked him up and scratched under his chin. For the first time that day, all the bad things went away. Mugsy loved chin scratches!

AHHHHH, chin scratch, chin scratch, chin scratch, ahhhhhhhh!

"Say good-bye, Mugsy!"

Mugsy opened his eyes. Tessa had suddenly lowered him so he was face-to-face with Thor. It was good that Mugsy was being held in midair. Otherwise, he knew he would have fallen over!

Pugs are known for their "wrinkled" faces.

Chapter 4
Obstacle Central

The week passed quickly. Before Mugsy could catch his breath, Tessa was telling him it was time for their second class.

She put him back in the shoulder bag, and off they went. Mugsy thought about the week. In some ways it had flown by. But the practice sessions went slowly. Mugsy tried hard, but he was easily distracted.

The phone was the scariest thing of all. It was always so loud and unexpected. Nothing startled him more. *R-I-I-I-N-G!* sent him straight up into the air.

R-I-I-I-N-G! He fell off the bed and broke a lamp on the way down.

R-I-I-I-N-G! He tumbled down the stairs and crashed into the table in the hall.

R-I-I-I-N-G! He landed on top of Tessa's mother's laptop—in her mother's lap.

Mugsy shook his head. He had to stop thinking about all his disasters. They made him feel really bad. He had other things to worry about.

★ ★ ★ ★ ★ ★

Tessa and Mugsy stood in their spot at Top Dog and waited for the second class to begin. He looked around the room. There were a lot of new things in the middle of the floor.

There were boxes stacked into stairs. There was a big standing hoop attached to a metal stand. There were many orange pyramids like he sometimes saw around holes in the sidewalk. There was a ramp that went up and one that went down. Before he could figure out what it was all about, someone said hello to them.

"Hi," replied Tessa. Mugsy looked up.

Oh, thought Mugsy, *she's talking to that boy we met last week, the one whose dog is a —* AAAUUUGGGHHHH!

Thor stood directly in front of Mugsy.

Mugsy scolded himself, *You have got to stop daydreaming! You just nearly walked into the jaws of death!*

"I saw you in the park this week," said Andy. He smiled at Tessa.

"Really? Do you live near there?"

Andy nodded. He kept smiling. "Right at Grand Street."

"Wow!" Tessa giggled. "We're neighbors!"

Just then Frank said, "All right, let's get started. This week, we're introducing the obstacle course."

There's that word again—obsti—obsticky—

"This is a great way for you and your dog to have fun. And it will help you practice basic obedience commands. We're going to—"

Obsti-*what?*

"Heeeeeyyyy!" A door slammed. Mugsy jumped.

"Let's get this party going!" screeched Zach.

"Sorry we're late," said Mrs. Egan.

Zach kept screeching. "We're late! We're late! We're so so so sorry! Hey! Who cares! I'm here!

I'm here! KI-KI-KI-KI!"

Zach raced to his place in line next to Kiki. Zach jumped back and forth over the top of Kiki. Kiki stood with Mugsy on one side and Zach on the other. Her head and tail were both held high in the air.

"Look who has a fan club."

Mugsy spun around. Thor was growling at Kiki. Mugsy suddenly realized Kiki was growling lowly back at Thor. Nobody else seemed to notice.

Why do I always end up in the middle? wondered Mugsy.

"So," said Frank.

His voice calmed the big dogs. The growling quieted, but Mugsy could still feel the tension.

Frank kept talking. "Girl will demonstrate the correct way to run the obstacle course. Girl?"

Mugsy heard the sound of a dog door flapping. He wondered where those magic doors were. He really wanted to be able to escape!

Suddenly, Girl came around the corner. She

trotted across the floor like a movie star. She was so confident, it made Mugsy feel proud to know her. When she turned and winked at him, a dog smile broke across his face.

Girl trotted to Frank's side. She sat down and looked up at him.

"Good, Girl," he said. Then, "Go!"

She was as graceful as a dancer. Girl glided over every object in the middle of the floor. Mugsy watched in awe. She went up and down the steps on her hind legs. She sailed into the air with all four legs tucked beneath and glided through the hoop. She went back around and leaped through the hoop again. This time, her legs were outstretched. Humans and dogs alike gasped.

Only one voice could be heard murmuring mean things.

"I can do that blindfolded," hissed Kiki.

"Ha!" chuckled Zach.

Girl zigzagged around the orange cones. She went up and down the ramps. She spun herself in circles and made a figure eight. At last, she came to the end of the course. She fell to her side and rolled over three times. She stood up and bowed with her front legs extended in front of her.

"Good, Girl!" Frank said. He patted her head. The humans applauded. The dogs looked at her with awe.

"That's all you have to do!" Frank said. The humans laughed. The dogs didn't.

★ ★ ★ ★ ★ ★

Over the next hour, every dog took their first turn on the obstacle course.

"Let me! Let me!" shrieked Zach. "Oh, yeah! I can jump! I can spin!"

Kiki stepped in front of Zach.

"You're right," Zach said suddenly. "You should be first. Absolutely! Kiki is first!"

Kiki turned in Thor's direction. She was smirking. Thor let out another low growl. Once again, Mugsy stood between the two big dogs.

One, two, three . . . Mugsy was trying to make himself disappear. He kept wiggling his nose and blinking his eyes. He'd seen it on TV. It had worked there. *Please, oh, please, let me disappear!*

Things only got worse. Zach did a good job on his first try. But Kiki was amazing.

Girl Says

German Shepherds are good at everything! These dogs are one of the smartest breeds. They are the chosen breed for many different jobs—search and rescue, police work, drug tracking, bomb detection, Seeing Eye, and herding. There doesn't seem to be a job they can't do!

Mugsy was surprised when Thor took his turn. Thor kept his head down. He didn't do any of the tricks. He just walked through the course silently. He didn't obey a single command.

I guess you don't need to do pet tricks when you own the jaws of death, Mugsy thought. *At least*

he's walking. I'll be happy if I can get my legs to walk!

Mugsy's turn finally came. He took a deep breath. He told himself he could do it. Then Frank said "Go!" and Mugsy fell over.

He could hear the other dogs laughing, especially Kiki and Zach. He saw Girl watching from the corner. She shook her head.

When class ended, Kiki walked by Mugsy. Zach was at her heels.

"You know what they have on my farm?" Kiki asked.

Mugsy looked around.

"Yes, Pug Boy, I'm talking to you," she said.

"Pug Boy! Ha! Pug Boy! Good one! Pug Boy!" squealed Zach.

Kiki shut Zach up with a single look. "As I was saying, we have these strange goats on my farm. We call them fainting goats. That's what you remind me of, Pug Mug. Whenever these goats get startled, their leg joints lock up and they fall over!"

"AAHHH!" howled Zach. "Fall right over! Fainting goats! Good one! Great one! The Pug's a goat! The Pug's a goat!"

Mugsy wanted to crawl under a rock. Kiki smiled a mean smile. Then she turned and put her tail in Mugsy's face. When she walked away, Zach followed.

Mugsy turned toward the other dogs. He hoped nobody else had heard Kiki. He didn't want to be known as "Goat Dog." The only dog staring at him was Thor.

Mugsy felt his legs freeze. He fell right over, just like the goats.

Chapter 5
From Bad to Worse

It had been a whole month since Mugsy's first class at Top Dog Obedience School. It wasn't getting easier. Every time Tessa said "Time for class!" Mugsy's heart raced.

He'd hide under the bed. He'd try to think of other ways he could prove he was a good dog. Maybe he could save someone's life. Maybe he could fight off a burglar.

"Okay!" Tessa announced. "Let's go do some tricks! This is your week, Mugsy!" Tessa said. "I can feel it. This week, you're going to go up those stairs! I know you can!"

How do you know that? Mugsy wondered.

★ ★ ★ ★ ★ ★

"Call me an Obsti-maniac!" cried Zach as Tessa and Mugsy arrived. "Who climbs the stairs? I do! Who clears the ring? I do! Who skates the cones? Uh-huh! You know it! I do!"

"Typical Jack Russell." Girl was behind Mugsy.

"Do you always have to sneak up on me?" Mugsy squeaked.

"Honey, I could stand in front of you with a spotlight on my head, and you'd still be surprised." Girl smiled.

Mugsy hung his head. He felt so ashamed. He was such a scaredy-cat.

"At least you're not like . . . that!" Girl pointed her nose in Zach's direction.

"STAND BACK and admire perfection!" Zach sang out.

"No," said Mugsy, almost admiring Zach's confidence even if it was annoying. "I'm definitely not *that*!"

"Come on, Mugsy!" Girl said. "You can do this. And in one month, you can prove it to the world!"

Mugsy turned toward Girl. "What?"

"Every term ends with a competition. You knew that, right?"

Mugsy yelped in surprise. He had forgotten

about the competition.

"It's just for fun," said Girl. "You win ribbons and there are lots of treats! You'll do great!" Girl continued. "Just remember you're a proud Pug!"

Girl Says

Pugs have a noble history! Pugs have been a favorite subject of many great painters. Nobles in the courts of Europe owned Pugs because they were thought of as "fashionable." And one Pug even acted as a secret messenger between Napoleon Bonaparte and his wife when she was in jail in Paris!
(They would send messages tucked inside the Pug's collar!)

"The point is," Girl said, "Pugs have a great history. You need to know that. You need to be proud of who you are and what you come from!"

Do we look proud?

"I am Mugsy," he said. "I come from under Tessa's bed."

"Keep working on it, kid." Girl smiled at him. She trotted away and disappeared around the corner.

A competition? Mugsy said to himself. *Why did she have to remind me? I'll never be brave enough to stand up in front of a crowd. I can't even stand in front of a mirror.*

"Okay!" Frank shouted. "Today we're going to add some tricks. Now that everybody has the basics under control . . ."

Excuse me? Mugsy thought. *I don't have* anything *under control!*

"We want the competition to be exciting, don't we?" asked Frank.

The humans nodded. Frank explained the new tricks. Mugsy stared at the floor.

"So," said Frank, "let's try to get each of the dogs up on their hind legs for just a step or two. Or, if it's just not right for your dog, try adding some rollovers to the end of the course."

No one was surprised when Zack walked on his hind legs on his first try, and Kiki did three rollovers in a row.

"Show-offs," growled Thor when Kiki and Zack walked by.

"Loser Pit Bull," said the German Shepherd.

"What's your special skill? Eating people?"

Mugsy slid down to his belly. He lifted his front paws up over his ears. He didn't want to see any blood. He was sure Thor was going to bite somebody's head off. He just hoped it wasn't his.

But when he looked up again, Thor was on the obstacle course. He went up and down the steps. He walked under the hoop. He did a circle around three of the cones and then lay down on his side before getting up.

"Nice try, Thor," Frank said.

Mugsy was amazed. Thor looked almost happy. *Does he really care about doing a good job on the obstacle course?* Mugsy wondered. But when he took another look, Thor's face had changed. He just looked mean again.

When it was Mugsy's turn, he tried to remember everything Girl had told him.

Pugs are amazing. Pugs are great. I am Napoleon. I am the queen of England.

Maybe his facts were a bit mixed up, but he felt a burst of courage. His legs started to move. He wasn't walking on his hind legs, but he didn't care — he was walking! He moved toward the stairs. His right foot lifted onto the first step. A hush fell over the room.

I am a proud Pug. I like to paint. I am fashionable.

He was two steps off the ground! Then he was on the top of the steps.

"YEEEEAAAAHHH!!" An enormous cheer rang out.

The sound was terrifying. Before he knew it, Mugsy was up in the air. He landed on his side and tumbled down the other side of the stairs.

"GOAT DOG strikes again!" screamed Zach. The Jack Russell sprang over Mugsy and ran the course again just to show off.

Mugsy shook his head. *So close,* he thought, *so close.*

"Thank you! Thank you! I'll accept all ribbons and trophies now. I'm Zach. I'm a Jack! I'm Zach! I'm a Jack!"

"SHUT UP!" Thor was standing in front of Zach. Zach stopped in his tracks. "Shut up and sit down before I do something you will regret!"

Every eye was on the Pit Bull.

"You want to start something?" Kiki stepped between Thor and Zach.

"Leashes," Frank commanded. All the humans quickly moved to get their dogs on their leashes. Girl was peeking through her dog door. "Alpha dogs," she mumbled.

As the dogs were pulled away by their owners, Tessa picked up Mugsy.

"You did great, Mugs," she whispered. "Don't let that stumble at the end get you down."

Andy stepped up to them. "Would you like to get together in the park this week?" he asked. "It seems like both our dogs could use some practice."

NNNNNNNOOOOOOOO! Mugsy screamed. But it did no good.

Tessa smiled. "That's a good idea," she said. She held Mugsy up to her face. "How about that, Mugsy? You and Thor are going to have a playdate!"

Another distinctive Pug feature is its curled tail.

Aren't we handsome?

Chapter 6
Endless Furprises . . .

"**M**ugsy?" Tessa's feet were right next to the bed. Mugsy had been living under the bed since the last class. He hoped it wasn't time for the playdate.

"You have to come out. Mom says you can't eat under the bed anymore. She also says you have to start going outside without me carrying you."

Tessa's voice sounded funny. She sounded scared.

"Mugsy?" Tessa was on her hands and knees, looking under the bed. "Mom said this is it," she said softly. "If you don't get some confidence and obey by the time class is over, she's sending you to the farm she found for homeless dogs."

Mugsy could see a tear in Tessa's eye.

"Now come on," she whispered.

Mugsy couldn't stand it. He couldn't bear making Tessa so sad. He put his fears aside and crawled out from under the bed.

"Good dog," she said with a smile. "I know you're a good dog."

Mugsy's heart leaped. *She knows I'm a good dog! She knows I'm a good dog!* He was overjoyed.

Tessa carried him downstairs and tucked him in the shoulder bag.

Tessa says she knows *I'm good! I'm good! I'm a good dog!*

They sped along on the bicycle.

I am not a bad dog. Not a terrible dog. He felt like dancing!

The bike slowed. Mugsy felt Tessa's hands lift him from the bag.

She knows I'm—AAAAUUUUGGGGHHHHH!

Thor! He hadn't realized they were already at the park! Tessa put him down right in front of Thor!

"Hi, Tessa!" Andy said.

"Hey!" said Tessa. "I think Mugsy's getting

better. He was calm all the way here!"

AAAAUUUUUUGGGGHHHHH! Mugsy screamed again inside his head. Then he fell onto his back.

"Maybe you spoke too soon," said Andy with a smile.

Thor stepped toward Mugsy. Mugsy's life flashed before his eyes. But nothing happened.

Slowly, he opened his eyes. He checked his body. He was still alive. His legs were all still working. He wondered why Thor hadn't eaten him yet.

Thor opened his mouth. Mugsy took a deep breath and shut his eyes again. *This is it!* he thought.

"I have to tell you," the big dog said, "it's a little annoying, you being so timid."

Mugsy opened one eye.

"I mean, I just stand around and wait to see when you'll fall over. It's like a counting exercise —how many times will he fall over today?"

Mugsy stared at Thor.

"On the other paw, I appreciate your being realistic about your situation. Most of you little guys—Zack the Jack, for example—don't seem to have any idea where you stand, which, by the way, is way down here."

Thor pawed at the ground. Mugsy nodded.

"Still . . . I have to say—snap out of it!"

Mugsy's eyes were as big as saucers.

"Stand on your own four feet. Get a grip! You'll end up getting shipped out if you don't get a handle on your nerves!"

Mugsy was stunned. He slowly rolled over to his side and stood up.

"Right," Mugsy said slowly. He couldn't believe he was talking to the Pit Bull. "You are absolutely right." He remembered Tessa's tears. He was about to get kicked out.

"Okay, you two!" Andy shouted. He and Tessa both threw a stick. The two dogs looked at their owners.

"Fetch!" they both said.

Thor looked toward the stick and then back to Andy.

"Go! Thor! Get the stick!"

Thor took a deep breath.
He started walking toward the stick.

"Run!" Andy shouted.

Thor pretended not to
hear him.

"You too, Mugsy!"
Tessa said. "Get the
stick."

Mugsy looked at Thor
and followed him.

Thor turned back to Mugsy. "As long as
we're setting the record straight," the big dog
said, "I'd appreciate it if you would stop acting
like I ate your best friend."

Mugsy nodded at Thor.

"I've never bitten anything but my dinner,"
Thor said. He sounded sad. "Yet people act like
I ate all the cats in the neighborhood."

"Wow," mumbled Mugsy.

"It's not easy being a Pit Bull," Thor said,
and then he stopped. "Nobody ever goes looking
for a Pit Bull when they want a new friend.

People 'ooh' and 'ahh' over little dogs like Pugs all the time. Nobody says 'aaaahhhhh' about a Pit Bull."

Girl Says

Pit Bulls get bad press! Pit Bulls will fight to the death if they're in a battle with another dog. But the truth about Pit Bulls is that they are wonderful dogs if raised to be gentle and well-behaved.

"I never thought of it that way," said Mugsy.

"Did you see where those sticks went?" Thor asked as he looked around the park.

Mugsy looked around. "I think those are them," he said.

"You're right," said Thor. "Nice work."

Mugsy couldn't believe it. The Pit Bull thought he'd done "nice work!"

"Thanks!" Mugsy said proudly.

With every throw, Thor and Mugsy moved a little quicker.

"Good dog, Mugsy!" Tessa cooed.

"Way to go, Thor!" exclaimed Andy.

The afternoon passed in the blink of an eye. Before Mugsy knew it, it was time to go home.

"You did great, Mugsy," Andy said. Mugsy felt like a strong dog.

"So did you, Thor!" Tessa said, and she patted the Pit Bull on the head.

Thor walked alongside Mugsy as they left the park. "So I'll see you at class, and you won't fall over, right?"

"I won't!" Mugsy said, and he smiled at Thor. "I will definitely stay on my feet."

"Good," said Thor.

"Now all we have to do is get Zach to shut up," Mugsy said.

"I know what will shut Zach *and* Kiki up!" Thor said.

"What?" Mugsy asked as they came to the edge of the park.

"We're going to beat them in the competition!" Thor said.

"We are?" Mugsy was amazed.

"We are. I've just decided. I want to win!"

Mugsy felt his legs freezing up. The fear of the competition caught him by surprise. But then he remembered his promise to his new friend. He wasn't allowed to fall over.

Mugsy took a deep breath and said, "Wow," and stood tall.

Chapter 7
A Brand-New Dog

Three days later, Mugsy walked into Top Dog on his own four feet.

"Gee, Mugsy," Tessa said quietly. "You're like a brand-new dog!"

Tessa was right. Mugsy was walking into class to meet his friend. He wasn't alone. He was ready to face the obstacle course and conquer it!

They walked into the big room. Mugsy looked around. He had so many things to tell Thor. Where was he? Where was his friend? Mugsy felt his bravery fading.

"Ready to spend another class on your back, Goat Dog?" someone hissed.

He turned and saw Kiki. She was smiling and baring her teeth at Mugsy.

I won't fall over, the Pug chanted to himself. *I won't fall over!*

"Hey, Goat!" screeched another voice. Zach appeared. He leaped back and forth over Kiki's back. "Faint lately?" Zach pretended to fall over himself. He and Kiki laughed loudly.

Mugsy could feel his legs stiffening. He knew what would happen next. He would fall over.

"Hey," said someone behind him. He snapped his neck around. "What's up, Mugsy?"

Thor stood looking at him.

"Goat Dog! Goat Dog!" teased Zach.

"Everything okay?" Thor asked.

Mugsy nodded. He felt the stiffness in his legs begin to fade. His bravery was returning.

"Good to see you, Thor," Mugsy managed. He could tell the Pit Bull was pleased. He liked having someone talk to him, too.

"Hey, Goat!" Zach taunted.

"He's not a goat!" Thor shouted. All the dogs went silent.

"Whatever, man," Zach said. "He's your Pug."

"He's not my Pug. He's his own Pug," snapped Thor again.

I'm my own Pug? wondered Mugsy. *That's amazing!*

"What's got your tail in a twist, Thor?" Kiki asked in a nasty tone. "Are you best friends with a Pug now?" The German Shepherd laughed. Mugsy stole a look at Thor. He wanted him to say, "Yes! Yes! Mugsy is my friend!"

But before anyone could say anything, Frank entered the room and class started.

★ ★ ★ ★ ★ ★

No one was surprised when Kiki and Zach took their turns on the obstacle course. Neither dog missed a trick. But when Thor took his turn, everyone was surprised.

The Pit Bull looked like a show dog. He stepped proudly over the stairs. He leaped into the air and through the hoop. Mugsy's jaw dropped. He was so proud of his friend. Thor kept moving. He hit every turn of the cones. He did the figure eight. Finally, he lay on his side and rolled over twice.

When he finished, the room was silent. Then everyone started cheering. Mugsy ran to Thor.

"Amazing!" Mugsy said.

Thor smiled at Mugsy. "Now it's your turn."

Mugsy walked bravely to the starting line. There was a gasp when he stood up on just two legs. He took four steps before coming back down on his front paws.

Just keep moving, he told himself. He moved over the steps. He took a deep breath and leaped into the air. He missed the hoop completely, but it didn't matter. He kept going. He moved in and out of the cones, then rolled over once.

Hey, thought Mugsy, *falling is kind of fun when you do it on purpose!*

The cheers were just as loud for Mugsy as they had been for Thor. Only Kiki and Zach sat silent.

"You're the best dog in the world!" Tessa cooed. She scooped him up and kissed him.

He licked her face and squirmed to get down. He was thrilled she was happy, but he wanted to talk to Thor.

"Okay! Okay!" She laughed. "You can get down!"

Mugsy raced over to Thor. Thor and Kiki were locked in a stare-down.

"I am not giving up that trophy," Kiki hissed. "Whatever you're trying to pull, you can forget it! You'll never be anything but a dumb Pit Bull."

Thor didn't speak. He just stared at Kiki. Kiki nudged Zach. The small dog took the cue.

"Yeah, right, right." Zach raced. "Sure! Oh, yeah! Like that's gonna happen! Like a Pit Bull and a Pug are really going to beat a German Shepherd and a Jack Russell. I'm so sure!"

"That's exactly what's going to happen!" roared Thor. He was so loud, it was like thunder.

Zach hid behind Kiki. Kiki smiled.

Mugsy couldn't believe it. It was like Kiki had wanted Thor to go after Zach. It was like she was happy Zach had pushed Thor to lose his temper!

Thor jumped past Kiki and tried to get to Zach.

"Stop, Thor!" Mugsy cried. "Stop!"

Girl Says

One leader only, please! All dogs are descended from wolves. Many of their behaviors can still be traced back to those origins. For example, they are "pack animals" just like wolves. Pack animals work as a group, and each group has one leader. When more than one dog thinks it's the leader, there can be trouble!

"Leashes!" Frank's voice sailed above the barks and shouts. All the humans scrambled to their dogs.

Mrs. Egan hurried over to Zach. "My sweet Zachy! Oh, dear! That big beast tried to eat my dog!"

"No! He didn't," pleaded Andy as he held

tight to Thor. "He just wanted your dog to back off a little."

Everyone backed away from Thor. Suddenly, Andy and Thor were all alone in the middle of the room.

"I'm afraid I can't allow that kind of behavior," Frank said sternly. Mugsy's head swung from human to human. He had to make them understand it wasn't Thor's fault.

"He's a powerful dog," Frank continued. "If he can't control himself around small dogs, he can't stay."

"He's a good dog . . ." Andy started, but his voice trailed off. He looked around the room. He could see how afraid everyone looked. "Never mind," he said quietly. "We'll go."

Thor stared at the floor. He looked so sad. It broke Mugsy's heart.

"Guess you won't be getting the trophy after all," Kiki snickered at Thor.

That's when Mugsy knew he had to do something.

"Mugsy!" Tessa's voice was filled with surprise.

Every dog and human head turned to see what was happening. The little Pug was on his feet. He glared at Kiki. Then he walked right up to Thor and sat down. Thor lifted his head slowly. When he saw Mugsy, he smiled.

"Well," exclaimed Tessa, "I guess he doesn't scare *all* the little dogs!"

Before anyone else could talk, a little Shih-Tzu and a big sheepdog joined them in the center of the floor.

"Look at that!" Andy cried.

"But he tried to eat my dog!" whined Mrs. Egan. "You mustn't allow him to stay!"

All eyes turned to Frank and waited to see if Thor was through.

I have to stand by my friend.

Chapter 8
Stepping Out

"Thor may return for the last class, Andy," Frank finally said. "But if there is any more trouble, he will not be allowed to compete."

"Thanks, Frank," Andy said with a smile. "Thanks a lot!"

"There's just one more class anyway," Mugsy whispered to Thor. "The next day is the competition. You just have to keep your cool around Zach. We can do this!"

"We?" asked Thor.

"Yeah!" Mugsy said. "You and me, Thor. We'll practice every night in the park."

"We will?"

"You bet! We're going to sneak out and meet in the park. We'll practice all the tricks so that by next week, we'll be the Kings of the Course!"

★ ★ ★ ★ ★ ★

Mugsy stepped quietly out the dog door. For

the first time ever, Mugsy was glad Tessa had shown him where the dog door was. He had never been brave enough to use it before. But the door made his whole plan possible.

As he cleared the door, the flap slapped down and made a loud noise. Mugsy froze. He listened hard for the sound of anyone stirring. The night was quiet.

He took off through his backyard. He got to the corner where the fence met the house. He slipped through the opening. He'd noticed the wide space a hundred times but never wanted to test it—until now. Mugsy ran down the sidewalk toward the park. It was easy! His heart was leaping out of his chest, but not from fear. Mugsy had never felt so excited and alive! He was running free in the middle of the night to meet his Pit Bull friend in the dark park!

Who am I? Mugsy asked himself. He made himself laugh. *Who am I, and what have I done with the real Mugsy?*

Thor was waiting for him just inside the stone walls of the park.

"Hey!" Mugsy called. "Did you have any trouble?"

Practice makes perfect.

"Nope," said Thor. "I nudged the cellar door, and it opened. It was a little tight in the crawl space—but here I am!"

Thor and Mugsy took off through the park. They knew they had to practice, but couldn't help taking a minute to run free. It felt so good!

They started finding things in the park that they could use for practice. The playground was the perfect spot. There were steps and ramps, and bars to jump over. Thor and Mugsy would go around and around. They would follow each other through the playground course. Then they would take turns watching each other and offering suggestions.

"It's only the first night," Mugsy said as they headed home, "and you're already better!"

"Thanks!" Thor said. "I appreciate your

saying that." The big dog looked away like he was a bit embarrassed.

"No problem!" Mugsy said. "I'll see you tomorrow!"

Girl Says

Agility training can work for any breed! Lots of breeds can succeed at agility training and obstacle courses. Working dogs tend to do best. But many breeds have done well in competition. Dogs that are built to move easily, jump well, and have good balance have a real advantage. German Shepherds, Jack Russell Terriers, and Boxers all have a history of doing well in competition. Though it's not common, there have even been some Pugs that have done well!

Every night the two dogs met at the park entrance. They would take off at top speed toward the playground. This was Mugsy's favorite part. He loved the feel of running faster than he ever knew he could. He loved feeling his ears flapping as he ran. He loved knowing the big dog up ahead was his friend.

The night before their last class, Thor and Mugsy practiced harder than ever.

"Try to get over the bar, Mugsy," Thor encouraged. "I think you can do it."

"Hello? I'm eleven inches tall," Mugsy said to Thor. "Have you forgotten how close to the ground I am?"

"No," Thor said. "But I still think you can do it. You bounce well."

"Well, thanks," Mugsy said. "I think."

"If I can control my temper," said Thor, "you can try to jump over a high bar."

"Is it really hard for you to control?" Mugsy asked his friend.

"I have some anger-management issues," Thor admitted. "But it's gotten easier recently."

Mugsy looked up at Thor. Thor was looking back at him. The two dogs smiled at each other.

Mugsy turned back to the course. He lowered his head and stared at the bar. He took off at top speed. Then he pushed off the ground with a mighty blast. He sailed into the air and over the bar.

Mugsy was so excited when he landed that he threw himself into the air again. He flipped around in a circle. He had done it, and his friend had seen it! The sound of Thor shouting was more glorious than a whole arena cheering.

★ ★ ★ ★ ★ ★

Tessa and Mugsy stood outside Top Dog Obedience School. For the first time, Mugsy couldn't wait to get inside. He pulled on his leash. Tessa laughed.

"Hold up, Mugsy!" she said. "I have something for you."

She reached into her pocket and pulled out a little piece of metal.

"I'll attach this to your collar later, but I wanted you to see it now. It's a charm for your collar, Mugsy."

Mugsy moved toward Tessa's hand. He

studied the charm.

"You know what it says?" Tessa asked.

Mugsy looked Tessa in the eyes.

"It says *I'm a Good Dog!* because you are!" She hugged Mugsy. He wanted to hug her back.

Just then, Kiki arrived.

"Goat Dog," she hissed as she walked by.

But Mugsy didn't flinch. Kiki wasn't going to win anymore—not on the obstacle course, and not as a bully, either!

Thor's performance in class that day gave Kiki even more reason to feel insecure. He sailed through every trick without a single mistake. Mugsy could see Kiki's eyes narrow from across the room. Mugsy jumped up and begged to go next. When he finished, there was a huge round of applause. He had done every trick except the hoop. It was higher than the bar on the playground, and he hadn't stretched up high enough. But even so, Kiki looked mad. She pulled Zach aside. Kiki pointed toward Girl. Then she pointed toward her doggy door. Then she glared at Thor and Mugsy.

"What do you think they're up to?" Mugsy whispered to Thor.

"I don't know," Thor answered. "But I'm sure she's planning something!"

Pugs once lived in the royal courts of Europe.

Chapter 9
Good Dog, Bad Dog

Mugsy barely slept that night. It was the night before the final competition, but also the first night all week he didn't meet Thor in the park. He missed his friend.

The next morning, it was a great relief when he finally heard Tessa stirring. He was at her bedside before she had her feet on the ground.

"My goodness, Mugsy." She smiled. "You're ready for your big day, aren't you?"

When they finally arrived at Top Dog, Mugsy leaped from the shoulder bag and ran to get through the doors.

"Mugsy!" Tessa cried, running behind him.

Mugsy looked around the room. Thor was already there. He ran to his friend.

"Mmm-mmmm-mmmm!" said Mugsy.

"Come again?" Thor said.

"Mm-mmmmmm-mm!" Mugsy repeated,

and then carefully laid something on the floor that had been in his mouth.

"Sorry," Mugsy said. "I have something for you. But it was in my mouth, so it was hard to tell you!"

"Take a deep breath, pal." Thor smiled. "You're acting like one of those crazy little dogs!"

"I *am* a crazy little dog," said Mugsy proudly. "But that doesn't mean I have to be a wimp." Mugsy looked up at Thor. "The same goes for you. Just because you are a big strong dog doesn't mean you're a bully."

Mugsy put his paw over the thing he had set on the floor. He slid the object across the floor to Thor. When he took his paw away, there sat the *I'm a Good Dog!* tag.

Girl Says

Rewards work wonders when training dogs! Few dogs have ever been taught a trick without the use of some kind of reward. It can be as simple as a pat on the head or as juicy as a piece of steak. Whatever you choose, the key is consistency. If you reward your dog for a good deed, do it every time.

"Tessa gave it to me, but I want you to have it," Mugsy said. "Because you have to remember, too—you're a good dog."

Thor looked away quickly. "Thanks," he said softly. Before he turned back to Mugsy, he brushed his face with his front paw. "That's nice of you. I'll be glad to wear it on my collar."

Mugsy nodded excitedly. "Okay! So have you seen Kiki or Zach? Do we know what they're planning yet?"

"I haven't seen them yet, but I'm sure we will."

"Mugsy!" Tessa called.

What are Kiki and Zack up to?

"I'll be right back," Mugsy said.

He dashed off through all the excited dogs. The room was crowded. There were lots of humans settling into chairs to watch the show.

"See, Mom!" Mugsy heard Tessa say. "See? He came right when I called him!"

Mugsy saw Tessa and her mom smiling at him. He decided to impress them. He sat down.

"Oh!" said Tessa's mother, and she put a hand to her cheek.

Mugsy felt like a genius.

★ ★ ★ ★ ★ ★

"Ready to fall on your face, you big Pit Bully?" Zach had snuck up on Thor.

Thor stared at him. He took deep breaths and told himself to stay calm.

"Who did you eat for breakfast today?" Zach asked as he inched closer.

Before Thor could respond, Zach darted at his feet and then ran away. When Thor looked down, he realized what had happened. Zach had stolen his present from Mugsy! Thor took off after Zach. Zach weaved through the people to the far side of the room.

"Excuse you!" a voice snapped.

Thor looked up ahead. Girl was shouting at Zach as he ran right under her. Thor swerved to avoid her.

Thor moved as fast as he could, but the little dog had the advantage in the crowd. He disappeared around the corner. When Thor finally rounded the corner, he saw where Zach had gone. Girl's doggy door was still swinging back and forth. Thor leaped. He aimed his front paws and head right through the door.

Suddenly, Thor was halfway into the other room. There was Zach, standing in the middle of the room. The tag was still in his mouth.

"Give me that tag!" Thor shouted. But then

he realized something worse.

Thor's head, front legs, and shoulders were inside the room with Zach. But the rest of him was still in the other room. . . . He was stuck.

"Guess you're a little fatter than a Boxer, Mr. Pit Bull . . . or should I call you Fat Bull?" Zach fell on his back and laughed hard.

"Welcome, ladies and gentlemen!" Thor could hear Frank starting the competition.

"Well, well." Zach giggled. "Good thing there's an Out door, or I'd have to miss the show." Zach stepped just outside of Thor's reach. "But missing the show is your job, Spit Bull," said Zach. "You're not going to be able to show off any of your tricks! *Toooo* bad!"

★ ★ ★ ★ ★ ★

"All the dogs have worked so hard over the last couple of months," said Frank. He was still talking to the audience. "Thank you for coming so they can show off their progress!"

"Where's Thor?" Andy rushed up to Tessa and whispered in her ear. "Have you seen him?"

"He was just here," Tessa answered.

69

Mugsy looked around frantically. *Where did he go? What happened?*

From the far end of the line, Kiki leaned forward and stared at the Pug. When Kiki saw Mugsy looking so panicked, she laughed. The only other dog watching was Girl.

Pugs can be apricot, fawn, black, or silver in color.

Chapter 10
Kings of the Course

"What's wrong?" Girl's familiar voice was behind Mugsy. "Why are you acting so antsy?"

Mugsy turned his head slowly. He didn't want anyone to notice him. Frank was still doing the introduction.

"Thor is missing!" Mugsy whispered.

"But I just saw him," Girl whispered back. "He was chasing—" Girl stopped speaking. She looked like she'd been struck by something. "Hold on," she whispered. "I'll be right back." She hurried away along the wall. She didn't want to attract attention. She was headed toward her doggy doors.

★ ★ ★ ★ ★

"Have a nice day, Pitiful—I mean, Pit Bull." Zach was still mocking Thor as he backed toward the Out door. "Sorry you won't be able to do—*anything*!" Zach was laughing as he put his head through the Out door.

The last thing he expected was what he saw.

"Going somewhere?" asked Girl.

"Yeah," said Mugsy, who stood next to Girl. "Didn't you forget something?"

For the first time in his life, Zach was speechless.

"Step away!" A snarling, snapping voice came from behind.

Mugsy and Girl spun around. Kiki was ready to pounce. She looked fierce.

"Let him go, and we won't have any problems. I am going to win this competition. I won't be stopped by a lazy Pit Bull, cowardly Pug, or stupid Jack Russell!"

Zach gasped. "Stupid Jack Russell . . . ?" His voice cracked.

"Don't be foolish," Girl said to Kiki. Her voice was calm, but Mugsy knew she was scared.

"Let the Terrier go so the competition can begin!" snapped Kiki as she lurched at Mugsy.

AAAUUUGGHH!

"Mugsy!" Tessa screamed. She ran to her dog. "What is going on here?"

Kiki growled at all of them, and Tessa screamed.

I can't believe this is happening.

"Kiki!" Frank rushed around the corner. He grabbed Kiki's collar. "This dog is disqualified!" said Frank.

Mugsy stared in disbelief. Girl barked her approval.

"You can't do that!" Kiki's owner cried. "She was just about to win!"

"Not when she's about to attack a dog and a person," Frank said.

"Hello? Excuse me!" came a muffled voice just as Andy arrived.

"What happened to my dog?" Andy exclaimed.

It was as if everyone had forgotten about Thor. They all ran into the other room.

"Kiki just got disqualified!" Mugsy barked at Thor.

"I know! I heard. Could someone get me out of here?"

"How did you get yourself into this mess?" Frank asked. He and Andy knelt next to Thor.

"Hey!" said Tessa. She walked over to Zach, who was suddenly the quietest dog in the room. She moved his front paw. "This is Mugsy's!" she said. She picked up the tag. "What are you doing with it?"

Zach looked away like he didn't hear anything.

Mugsy went to Tessa and took the tag in his mouth. He walked directly to Thor and set it down in front of his big friend.

"You gave it to Thor?" Andy asked in amazement.

"I think he did," said Tessa. "And I think Zach stole it from Thor."

"Well, all I can say is my little Zach wouldn't have done anything wrong if it hadn't been for that mean Kiki!" Mrs. Egan had just arrived. "That dog was a bad influence! Come to me, Zachy! I know you're a good boy!"

Finally, with help, Thor wriggled free.

"Now," Frank said, "let's get this show going!"

But Thor dashed from the room. He ran to the front doors where Kiki stood, about to leave. He jumped between her and the door. Mugsy ran to catch up.

"I'm going to beat you fair and square," Thor said to Kiki.

The other dogs gathered around Thor and Kiki. It was clear they all wanted Kiki to compete. They all wanted a chance to beat her in a fair contest. Frank crossed his arms and shook his head.

"Fine," Frank finally said. "Kiki can compete, but I don't want to hear a single growl."

Applause broke the silence, and the show began.

★ ★ ★ ★ ★ ★

The first six dogs performed well. No one messed up. There was no room for mistakes today.

"Zach the Jack Russell Terrier!" Frank announced.

The pressure was too much for Zach. Mugsy had never seen him so quiet. He stumbled through the course. He completely missed the hoop. Zach was a washout!

"Wow," said Mugsy nervously. "He really fell apart!"

"That's because he was all hot air," Thor said. "You've been working hard, Mugsy. You are rock solid!"

"Kiki the German Shepherd!" Frank said, and now the crowd went quiet. Kiki actually looked scared.

"I know it's crazy, but I feel bad for her," Mugsy whispered. "Nobody's rooting for her."

Thor looked at Kiki, then at Mugsy. The Pit Bull lifted his head and said, "Go, Kiki!"

There was a gasp from the crowd. Kiki froze. Her eyes glazed over with confusion. Thor's kindness was more than she could handle. She walked right past the hoop. She knocked over three cones. She did one roll at the end and then walked the wrong way off the course. Kiki was through.

"It's just us now," Mugsy said. "We're the only ones left."

"You want that trophy, Mugsy?" Thor asked.

Mugsy didn't know what to say. He knew Thor really wanted it, too.

"I have an idea!" Thor said, and he whispered into Mugsy's ear.

★ ★ ★ ★ ★ ★

"And now, ladies and gentlemen, we have only two dogs left. They have both come a long way. Amazingly, if either of these dogs performs his best today, he could walk away with the trophy."

Before Frank could introduce one name or the other, Mugsy and Thor burst through the crowd as a team. They leaped into the obstacle course and began to do all the tricks—together. They were like dancers as they went up and down the stairs on their hind legs. They floated through the air twice so that each had a chance to sail through the hoop. They danced around the cones, and up and down the ramp. Then they both fell to their sides and rolled three times. They rose to their feet and bowed together.

The crowd jumped to its feet and cheered in approval.

Tessa and Andy threw their arms into the air and ran toward their dogs.

"Yeah, Mugsy!" Tessa cheered.

"Way to go, Thor!" Andy shouted.

Mugsy and Thor looked at each other as the crowd chanted their names.

"Big Bully," Mugsy said to Thor with a smile.

"Little Wimp!" Thor shot back.

Then they both laughed and barked in victory.

Friends . . .

. . . to the end!